THIS BOOK BELONGS TO

For Hollie —LB
For Ali and Sarah —RLO

For Molly —David O'Connell

[Imprint]
MAKE YOUR MARK

A part of Macmillan Publishing Group, LLC
120 Broadway, New York, NY 10271

DAVE THE UNICORN: TEAM SPIRIT. Text copyright © 2019 by Egmont UK Ltd.
Illustrations copyright © 2019 by David O'Connell. All rights reserved.
Printed in the United States of America by LSC Communications, Harrisonburg, Virginia.

Library of Congress Control Number: 2019948847

ISBN 978-1-250-25636-2 (hardcover) / ISBN 978-1-250-25637-9 (ebook)

Our books may be purchased in bulk for promotional, educational, or business use.
Please contact your local bookseller or the Macmillan Corporate and Premium Sales Department at
(800) 221-7945 ext. 5442 or by email at MacmillanSpecialMarkets@macmillan.com.

Book design by Lizzie Gardiner

Special thanks to Liz Bankes and Rebecca Lewis-Oakes

Imprint logo designed by Amanda Spielman

Originally published in Great Britain by Egmont UK Limited in 2019

First American edition, 2020

1 3 5 7 9 10 8 6 4 2

mackids.com

HALT
If you dare harm this book
You will lose
All team spirit
And never win a game again
Even Monopoly

DAVE THE UNICORN

TEAM SPIRIT

PIP BIRD
ILLUSTRATED BY DAVID O'CONNELL

[Imprint]
MAKE YOUR MARK
New York

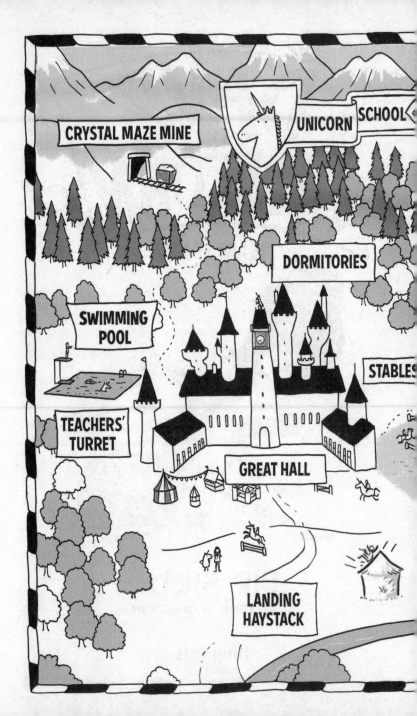

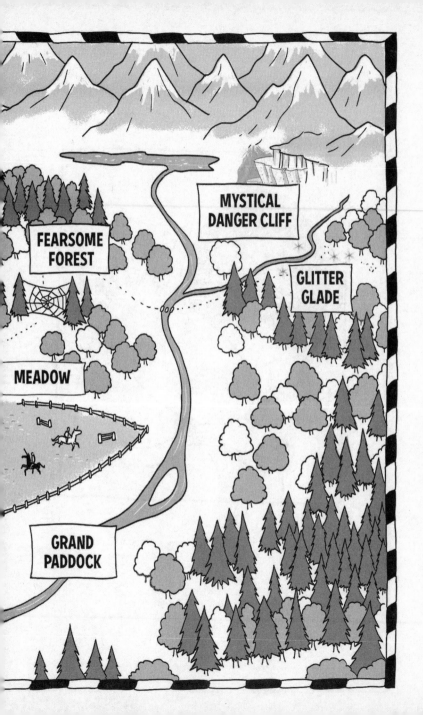

Contents

CHAPTER ONE
Back to Unicorn School

Mira Desai had been in the kitchen since five A.M. doing her homework.

Usually this would be a very strange thing to do, but Mira's homework was for Unicorn School and was much more fun than normal homework, so she wanted to spend every spare moment she had on it. The students had been asked to make a present for their unicorn, and Mira had thought of the PERFECT present for her unicorn, Dave. She was making him a lunch box. Dave loved lunch. And breakfast . . . and dinner!

Dave wasn't everyone's idea of the perfect unicorn—and he wasn't what Mira had been expecting when she'd dreamed of going to Unicorn School. He was plump, with stumpy little legs and a mane like straw that stuck up in all directions. And Dave was a little 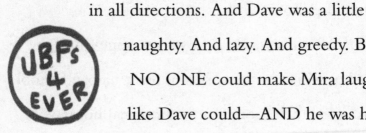 naughty. And lazy. And greedy. But NO ONE could make Mira laugh like Dave could—AND he was her UBFF (Unicorn Best Friend Forever). Nothing could change that.

Right now she was decorating the special lunch box with pictures of all the fun they'd had on her last trip to Unicorn School.

Mira was just writing Dave's name in glitter

when her sister, Rani, joined her in the kitchen. Rani was two years older than Mira and also went to Unicorn School. She was in Class Yellow, while Mira was in Class Red. (The classes went up through all the colors of the rainbow.) Rani's unicorn was named Angelica, and Rani always went on and on about how special and sparkly she was and how they'd won lots of medals. Rani laid a piece of paper on the table and put her fluffy pencil case next to it. She was making a poster to go on Angelica's stall door. She started carefully drawing her unicorn with a gel pen.

"I'm just drawing a picture of the time Angelica and I won THREE medals in ONE DAY," Rani announced.

Mira looked at the side of the lunch box.
She had stuck on a picture of the time Dave had
eaten three cakes in one minute.

"What's that?" said Rani, leaning over. "It looks
like a blob eating some other blobs. And why
have you drawn a rat?"

"That's ME," said Mira angrily.

Rani continued, "It's actually easier for you,
you know. Everyone is SO jealous of me having
a perfect unicorn. But no one would want your
unicorn—everyone knows he's the naughtiest,
awfulest unicorn in the world."

Mira shook her head. Rani had *no* idea about
the adventures she'd had with Dave. They'd made
it all the way through the Fearsome Forest AND

performed a daring rescue on the Mystical Danger Cliff. Mira turned to her sister. "*Awfulest* isn't a word," she said.

They kept drawing in silence. A little later, Mira and Rani's mom and dad came downstairs. "It's so wonderful that they have this experience to share," said Dad.

Then Mira grabbed Rani's pink gel pen and Rani put Mira in a headlock, so Mom had to separate them. She told them to get their bags and get in the car—it was time to go back to Unicorn School!

ᴜᴜᴜ

Mira was so excited that she could hardly keep still as they drove to the Magic Portal that would take them back to Unicorn School. It wasn't just that she would get to see Dave, but she'd also get to see her new Unicorn School friends Darcy and Raheem, too. The three of them had become great friends in their first semester at Unicorn School, when they'd all gone on a special quest to rescue their classmates.

6

Mom's car pulled up in the rec center parking lot, and the two girls immediately leaped out and ran over to the bush that hid the Magic Portal. Mom followed behind, carrying their bags, their homework, and one of Mira's shoes.

"You might need these!" she said.

"Thanks, Mom," said Mira, as Rani jumped up and down, impatient to go into the portal. Mira's hands were shaking, and she almost couldn't tie the laces on her sneakers. Mira had gotten brand-new glitter sneakers for her birthday from her parents. She LOVED them, and she couldn't wait to show them to Dave. (Even though Rani said Mira had copied her, since Rani had gotten *her* glitter sneakers first.)

After hugging Mom goodbye and taking the obligatory "off to school" photo, the two sisters crawled into the bush toward a patch of shimmering light. And after Rani told Mira to "stop hogging the portal," they reached out toward the sparkles and tumbled forward, into what felt like thin air. It had only been a few weeks since Mira had last done this, but she'd forgotten how fast it was! It was like going down the big slide at a water park, but with air whooshing around you and rainbow lights whizzing past. Mira and Rani giggled and held on to each other as they shot through the air and landed with a soft *thump* on the Landing Haystack, in front of the Great Hall.

"Bye!" said Rani, running off.

"MIRA!" came a shriek, and Mira
turned to see Darcy. Darcy shouted
"Woo-hoo!" and fluffed her big curly hair,
then gave Mira a jazz-hand high five. Raheem
was behind her, looking a little anxious as
he always did, but pleased to see Mira.

"We've been waiting for you to arrive

before we go and get our unicorns!" Raheem said, grinning.

That gave Mira a happy, warm feeling inside. Although she had friends in the real world, it was so nice to have special friends at Unicorn School to share lots of adventures with! The three friends started to talk about the presents they had made for their unicorns.

"I made this for Brave," said Raheem. "I'm a little worried he won't like it." And he held up a red cape with a blue felt *B* sewn onto it.

"He *will* love that, Raheem—it's so cool!" Mira said.

"I got Star a wig so that we can have matching hair," said Darcy.

As they approached the Grand Paddock, they heard a loud neigh and the thundering of hooves. Raheem's unicorn, Brave, was galloping toward them. Raheem instinctively dived behind a trough just as Brave skidded to a halt. Brave was confused for a moment, but then Raheem quickly crawled out and gave him a hug. Mira was right—Brave LOVED the gift. Raheem put it on him, and Brave stomped around, striking superhero poses.

Darcy and her unicorn, Star, were busy taking selfies with their matching hair. Mira looked around for Dave, until she saw a very familiar unicorn butt poking out from the fence surrounding the stables. Dave had gotten stuck in the fence trying to get to a pile of apples stacked

outside the cafeteria. When he heard Mira call his name, he whinnied. So Mira ran over. She tried pulling his legs to help get him out, but he remained stuck in the fence. She climbed over and gave him a shove from the other side.

With a loud *POP*, Dave came free from the fence and fell backward, knocking over a unicorn who'd been walking past.

"Sorry!" called Mira, as the unicorn picked herself up, tutted at Dave, and trotted away.

Mira turned back to her unicorn, who was trotting straight back toward the gap in the fence, eyeing the apples hungrily.

"Wait—Dave, I got you something!" said Mira, pulling the lunch box out of her bag.

Dave's eyes went wide and he gave a happy grunt. He was even more delighted when he nudged the lid off with his nose and saw that Mira had filled the lunch box with doughnuts. He scarfed them down immediately,

just as Mira

had expected

he would,

but he did a little trick of bouncing each doughnut on his nose before catching it in his mouth, which made Mira laugh.

"I don't think people realize how clever you are," said Mira, scratching behind his ears. Being back at Unicorn School was . . .

THE BEST!

CHAPTER TWO
Team Sloth!

"Good morning, Class Red," said Miss Glitterhorn.

"Good mooorrrrning, Miss Glitterhoorrrn," chorused Mira's class. They were sitting in their classroom. Each desk had a taller unicorn desk next to it, with a bag of hay and shelves for grooming brushes. As usual, Dave had already eaten his entire bag of hay and was sneaking mouthfuls from the desk next to them, which belonged to Jake and his unicorn, Pegasus.

Pegasus noticed and moved the bag away from

Dave with his hoof. Dave waited until Pegasus looked away and moved it back. Pegasus snorted indignantly. "Control your unicorn!" hissed Jake.

Mira wanted to remind Jake how she and Dave had rescued him from the Mystical Danger Cliff, but somehow she knew that wouldn't help. Dave ALWAYS managed to get on the wrong side of Jake, and she suspected Jake was embarrassed that Dave had come to his rescue.

Jake and Pegasus turned back to face the front, and Dave crept over to steal another mouthful of hay.

Miss Glitterhorn said she had some VERY important news for the class, which she would tell them right after she'd taken attendance.

"I wonder what it is!" squeaked Flo, her glasses falling off in excitement. Flo was unicorn obsessed and was wearing a unicorn onesie. Mira wasn't sure if it counted as dressing sensibly (Unicorn School Rule 20), but the onesie did look cool.

"Maybe it's a school trip," said Freya, who was Flo's twin sister.

Mira hoped that whatever it was, there would be a chance for her and Dave to win a medal. She had a ways to go to catch up with her sister's total of a hundred thousand million.

Attendance seemed to take FOREVER as the class all waited for the very important news.

FINALLY their teacher finished and said,

"Now, Class Red, I am excited to tell you that tomorrow is . . . Unicorn School Field Day!"

There were murmurs of surprise and then cheers from most of the class, except Raheem, who just fidgeted in his seat.

"What sports will we be playing?" asked Freya. Mira noticed that Freya had really perked up at the news, but her unicorn, Princess, looked horrified.

"Can we play handball?" said Darcy.

"Chess?" Raheem said hopefully.

"What about wrestling?" said Freya eagerly. Princess fainted.

"You don't get to pick the sports," said Miss Glitterhorn, raising her voice over the chatter.

"Now, in assembly we will be getting into our teams. The whole school will be divided into four teams, so you will be on a team with children from the other classes."

Mira wondered if she would end up on a team with her sister. She wasn't sure if it would be worse to be with Rani or competing *against* her.

"And the winning team," continued their teacher, "will get to go on a mystery quest."

An excited "Oooooooooooh" ran around the classroom.

Mira looked at Dave. *Maybe he's athletic in a secret and unexpected way*, Mira tried to tell herself.

But she couldn't forget what her sister said

that morning about Dave being the naughtiest, awfulest unicorn in the world.

Would they let their team down?

UUU

Mira looked at her team in the assembly hall. She was feeling more excited about field day now. The whole school had been divided up into four teams. Mira and Rani weren't on the same team, which was a relief. Rani was on a team with Jake, from Mira's class, who had spent the whole morning telling everyone how his parents had won Unicorn School Field Day every year and reminding everyone that they were Olympic show jumpers. Mira could hear Rani confidently telling the rest of the team that they were SO

going to be the winners. "And we HAVE to beat Mira's team," Rani declared. "Whatever it takes—do anything you can to win!"

Mira gulped and turned back to her own team.
She was with Raheem and Flo from Class Red,
and there were children from each of the other
classes. The team took turns saying their name
and the name of their unicorn. It was a *lot* of
names to remember. Mira already knew Jimmy
and Anja from Class Yellow, because they were
friends with her sister. There was a girl from
Class Green named Ali and a girl from Class
Blue named Sarah, and two boys from Class
Orange who were both named Tom and wore
matching T-shirts. Yusuf from Class Indigo
had a unicorn named Storm, who was inky
black and covered in silver dots that looked
like glittery raindrops. Their team captain was

a girl named Yasmin from Class Violet.

Flo was beside herself with excitement, and Miss Glitterhorn had to keep taking her outside to calm down. Raheem was the opposite— he stood there with his hands in his pockets, looking glum.

"It'll be fun, Raheem!" said Mira.

He frowned. "It's just that I'm really bad at all sports, and I don't want to let anyone down." He looked sideways at Brave, who was stretching and trotting on the spot.

"Don't worry," said Mira. "Winning doesn't matter. I mean, if we do win and get tons of medals and beat my sister and laugh in her face, that will be THE BEST . . ." Mira's voice trailed off as she pictured this.

"Mira?" said Raheem. He waved his hand in front of her face.

"Sorry—yes! The main thing is we all work together and have fun." She gave Raheem a friendly nudge on the shoulder.

Brave gave him a friendly nudge, too. Unfortunately, Brave often didn't realize his own strength, and Raheem went flying, landing in the middle of the next team.

Raheem untangled himself and came back over. Despite looking a bit dazed, he grinned at Brave. Mira could tell he appreciated his unicorn trying to cheer him up. Raheem cheered up even more when he saw that Sarah from Class Blue had brought a crossword book with her.

Madame Shetland, the tiny Unicorn School principal, announced that each team needed to think of a team name.

"All the teams are to be named after animals," the principal said, "so think very caref—"

"**SLOTHS!**" screamed Flo.

"Sloths," said Miss Glitterhorn, writing it down on a clipboard. Laughter from the other teams rippled around the hall.

"But—" said Mira.

"Be quiet, Sloths!" barked Madame Shetland. "Now, the rest of you, think very carefully about your team name and what it says about you and your ambitions."

After conferring, one team picked Cobras, Jake and Rani's team chose Rhinos, and Darcy's team spent so long arguing that they ended up being called Team Lions or Tigers.

"Why did you pick sloths?" Mira asked Flo.

"I heard they like hugs," said Flo, shrugging.

Mira sighed. Sloths were cute, but they didn't sound like the sort of animals who would come first at field day.

CHAPTER THREE
Bungee Wrestling

Madame Shetland returned to the front of the hall. She announced that each team had to come up one by one to collect their rainbow tracksuits. These were to be worn throughout field day, and there was only one for each of them so they had to GUARD THEM WITH THEIR LIVES.

"What do you think, Dave?" said Mira, as Team Cobra went to get their tracksuits. "Are we going to win?"

Dave cocked his head to one side, as if he was thinking, and then unleashed a giant heap of poop

onto the ground. Mira sighed and went to look for a poop shovel. So far, Dave didn't seem like he was about to reveal any surprising athletic abilities.

Just as she was making her way back, Rani and Jake walked past on their way to get their tracksuits.

"In fact," Jake was saying, "my mom got the school record for—

WWwwooOOaaarrghh!"

"What's woargh?" said Flo. "I've never heard of that sport."

Jake and Pegasus had both slipped on Dave's giant poop. Jake looked in horror at his sneakers. "They're really expensive!" he said.

"Sorry—I was just getting a shovel," said Mira, running over.

Dave gave a whinny that sounded exactly like a laugh. Jake narrowed his eyes.

"I'm glad your stupid unicorn isn't on MY team," he said.

"Well . . . I'm glad we're not on YOUR team!" said Mira. She looked around at her team for support. Raheem was helping Sarah with her crossword. Flo's unicorn was running around in circles chasing her own tail, while Flo was also running in circles chasing the tail of her unicorn onesie. The rest of them didn't seem to have heard. Except Brave, who marched over and stood behind Mira. He snorted loudly.

Rani laughed. "Maybe you should take a look at your team—they're obviously the rejects. We have *real* sports people on ours. Tanya from Class Green is practically on the US Women's soccer team."

"Actually, we have real sports people on our team, too!" Mira blurted out.

"Who?" said Rani, folding her arms.

Mira looked around at Team Sloth again. "Them!" she said, pointing at Tom and Tom from Class Orange, who were sitting the farthest away so were the least likely to hear.

"What sport?" said Jake, raising his eyebrows.

"Um," said Mira. Suddenly she couldn't think of ANY sports! "Bungee . . . wrestling?"

"Bungee wrestling?!" said Rani.

"Yes, bungee wrestling." Mira looked around. The boys had seen her pointing at them, and now they were coming over! "Anyway!" said Mira quickly. "*Wonderful* chatting with you." She wasn't sure why she'd started talking like her mom. "Bye!"

Dave popped up between Brave's legs and blew a raspberry.

"What*ever*," said Rani. "Your team is still awful. Because you've got the world's naughtiest, laziest, AWFULEST unicorn, and I don't care that's not a word!"

There was a gasp from the Sloths. Flo and her unicorn stopped running in circles, but then they became overwhelmed by dizziness and fell over. By now the two Toms had arrived at Mira's side.

"I pulled a muscle sitting down," said Tom 1.

"Me too," said Tom 2. "I think my butt's broken."

Rani gave Mira one last look of triumph, and then Team Rhino walked away, Jake and Pegasus trying to wipe the poop off their feet as they went.

"Dave," said Mira, as she watched Rani go. "We have to prove Rani wrong. We're going to COME FIRST at field day!"

She turned to her Unicorn Best Friend Forever. He was asleep.

∪∪∪

SCRREEEEEEEEEEEEEEEcccccCHHH!!!

Mira sat bolt upright in bed. Her alarm sounded different than usual. She looked around

the dorm room, which she was sharing with the rest of Team Sloth. The others were rubbing their eyes and looking startled.

ScrEEeeeeeeeeeEEECHHH!

The noise was even louder this time, and Mira nearly leaped out of bed in surprise. Their PE teacher, Miss Hind, was outside the window of the dorm blowing her whistle.

"Team Sloth—you are LATE!" the teacher shouted. "It's nine A.M."

Panic gripped Mira. How could they all have overslept? She set the alarm clock! She picked it up. It still said seven thirty. HOW HAD THIS HAPPENED?

Team Sloth scrambled out of bed and to the stables to collect their unicorns.

When Mira went into Dave's stall, he was hiding under a pile of hay.

"Come on, Dave—it's field day!"

Dave squeezed his eyes shut tighter and did a very fake snore.

Eventually, Mira bribed him out with some energy bars.

"You'll love field day," she said, as he trotted along next to her. Dave gave her a sideways look and raised his eyebrows.

"Where have you been?" said Darcy, wheeling over from Team Lions or Tigers as Mira and her teammates finally made it out onto the sports field. "We've been out here for an hour! Star and I performed all of *The Lion King* to get everyone in the mood."

"Weren't you supposed to be practicing sports?" said Raheem.

"Probably." Darcy shrugged.

"My clock stopped!" said Mira. She couldn't

believe they'd missed a whole hour of preparation.

"It's okay," said Flo, appearing behind Mira. "I've made up a cheerleading dance. Now we'll definitely win! Sparkles and I practiced it at midnight for five hours." Sparkles blinked blearily next to Flo, then swayed and fell into the long jump pit, fast asleep.

"Team Sloth—so good of you to decide to join us," said Madame Shetland icily. "May I ask why you are all wearing pajamas?"

They looked at one another. They had all forgotten to change into their rainbow tracksuits!

"Oh NO!" cried Mira, and she turned and

39

sprinted back toward the PE locker room. The rest of Team Sloth wandered slowly after her.

"Quick!" called Mira, as she raced into the locker room. But then she gasped. All the Team Sloth pegs were empty. Their tracksuits were gone!

The rest of the team joined her. They looked all around the locker room, but they couldn't find the tracksuits ANYWHERE. They ran out of the locker room and into the corridor, where Miss Hind was blowing furiously on her whistle to get them to hurry up.

"Why are you STILL not dressed?" she growled. They told her that the tracksuits had vanished.

Miss Hind folded her arms and frowned.

"It's not our fault! They really have disappeared," said Mira. "We looked everywhere!"

Miss Hind sighed and told them to follow her. She marched them to the PE closet, where they had to get spare PE outfits out of the lost-and-found bin. When they'd gotten changed, they looked RIDICULOUS. Everything was either too big or too small, or filthy or just *weird*.

"I can see why someone 'lost' these . . . ," said Mira, pulling on an enormous pair of shorts.

"Count yourself lucky!" said Raheem, who was wearing a tiny tank top with a picture of a rabbit on it, which had clearly been dyed pink in the wash.

CHAPTER FOUR
The Egg-and-Spoonicorn Race

As Team Sloth approached the sports field for the second time, Mira could see that the other teams were huddled together, stretching and warming up. Mira took a deep breath and told herself not to worry—maybe the extra hour and a half's sleep would mean Team Sloth had EVEN MORE energy stored up.

Maybe.

"Oh—you look . . . how unusual," said Miss Glitterhorn when she turned around to see

Mira, with the rest of Team Sloth trudging behind.

"Our tracksuits were gone," said Mira miserably.

Miss Glitterhorn started to reassure her that no one would notice, but she was drowned out by the sound of other teams collapsing into hysterics. Mira could hear her sister cackling louder than anyone.

At least I still have my glitter sneakers, Mira thought, trying to block out the laughter.

Mira asked Team Captain Yasmin if they should start warming up. Yasmin shrugged. So Mira decided to take charge. She was determined to show everyone that Dave wasn't naughty or lazy and that Team Sloth could do it, tracksuits or no tracksuits!

"Okay, team," said Mira. "Shall we do some stretching?"

There were a few murmurs from the team and someone yawned. Mira decided to take this as a YES.

"Okay!" said Mira, and then Ali from Class Green put her hand up.

"What are we doing again?"

"Stretching," said Mira. Tom 1 put his hand up.

"Can I go to the bathroom?"

"Can I go, too?" said Tom 2.

"Um, yes?" said Mira, unsure if she was allowed to give permission for this. "So—stretching! Stand on one leg and hold your ankle. NO, the other ankle!"

Three members of Team Sloth had fallen over, and they took the rest of the team down with them, ending up in a tangled heap on the grass.

"Um—warm-up done!" called Mira.

She felt like they should round things off with an inspirational pep talk. She asked Team Captain Yasmin if she wanted to do one, but Yasmin was reading a magazine. So it was up to Mira. She had never given a pep talk before. Sometimes when her mom went to her gym class she would have to take Mira with her, and Mira would sit in the corner and read. The man in charge of the class, who was named Tank, would shout things to encourage everyone to try harder or to stop them from leaving.

"Right, you lazy bunch of WEAKLINGS!" Mira shouted. "Get those PUNY BODIES into gear! Let's show those Cobras and Rhinos and

Lions or Tigers what we're made of and then
DESTROY THEM! We'll CRUSH them under
our feet and hooves! We'll—"

Miss Glitterhorn was passing by and said
it was great that Mira was motivating her team,
but perhaps she could be a bit more positive and
use less violent imagery.

"But you're all AWESOME," Mira continued.
Miss Glitterhorn nodded approvingly. "And just
as long as we crush my sister's team, that's all that
matters! Go Team Sloth!"

There was cheering from Flo, a thumbs-up
from Raheem, and a supportive fart from Dave.

SCRREEEeeeeeeeeeeeeeCHHH!

Miss Hind was blowing her whistle again: It was time for the first event.

∪∪∪

"Field day begins with the 'fun' events," growled Miss Hind. She was reading from a piece of paper and didn't sound as though she thought the fun events were very fun. "Remember, it's not the winning that's important—it's about teamwork. Apparently."

"The main thing is that everyone tries their best," piped up Miss Glitterhorn. "And that you all have FUN!"

She was drowned out by a boy from Team Cobra and a girl from Team Rhino, who were shouting "You're DEAD!" and "You're MORE

49

DEAD!" back and forth at each other.

Miss Glitterhorn showed them the scoreboard. There were columns for all four teams and spaces to put their points from each event. In the morning were the fun events: the Egg-and-Spoonicorn Race, the Magical Mystery Pouch Race, and the Hoop-onto-the-Unicorn-Horn Throw. Then there was a break before the serious sports events: the Long Jump and the Uni-Pole Vault. And after lunch there was the Cross-Country Obstacle Race.

Points would be given for each event, and the team with the most points would win the field day trophy, which was locked away in a cabinet next to the scoreboard.

TEAM COBRA	TEAM LIONS OR TIGERS	TEAM RHINO	TEAM SLOTH

Mira had heard Jake say that the trophy was MASSIVE and made of solid *glitter* gold. "That's why they lock it away," he said. "There's tons of stuff in my house made of glitter gold, and we have spies and dogs to guard it."

But, of course, what everyone was MOST excited about was that the winning team would be going on a mystery quest.

The teams were all mixed up into smaller

groups and would take turns in each event. Mira was doing the Egg-and-Spoonicorn Race first. In this race they had to sit on their unicorns and trot along, while the unicorns held the eggs on spoons in their mouths. Mira, Raheem, Flo, Yusuf, and Anja made their way to the starting line.

"Actually, it's very interesting," Raheem was saying. "It's all about the angle of the egg on the spoon—not about going fast." Brave snorted in disappointment. Raheem spent a few minutes adjusting the position of the spoon in his unicorn's mouth before reaching for the egg. "Hey—my egg's broken!"

"Oh, Raheem—you haven't even started the race yet!" said Miss Glitterhorn.

"No, I didn't break it!" Raheem protested.
"It must have already been like that—I've been
handling it VERY CAREFULLY!"

There were murmurs and calls of "Yeah right!"
from the other teams. But Miss Glitterhorn gave
Raheem the benefit of the doubt and a new egg.

Mira looked more closely at her own egg,
perched on the spoon in Dave's mouth. It was
cracked, too! She jumped off Dave and waved to
get Miss Glitterhorn's attention.

"I'm not giving out new eggs willy-nilly,
Mira," said the teacher, shaking her head.

"But—it's broken!" said Mira,
holding out the egg. Then Dave ate it.
Now she definitely needed a new egg.

"Make sure you take better care of this one," said Miss Glitterhorn, as she reached into her spare egg carton. Mira was about to say that this was unfair, but then she was distracted by shouts from the other teams. Dave was walking along the starting line, calmly eating the eggs off all the spoons.

Miss Glitterhorn withdrew the new egg and

disqualified Mira and Dave from the Egg-and-Spoonicorn Race.

And so Mira could only watch and cheer from the sidelines as Miss Hind blew her whistle, and they were off! Flo and her unicorn dropped their egg immediately, but they finished the race and got a point for effort. Raheem made Brave go extremely slowly, so their egg survived, but they finished five minutes behind everyone else and received no points.

The other members of Team Sloth did just as terribly. It turned out that their eggs were also broken before the race started—or in Yusuf's case, that the egg was massive and wouldn't fit on the spoon.

The other teams thought they were just complaining because they were losing, and Madame Shetland said that a bad worker blames their tools . . . but Mira couldn't help but think that something funny was going on.

CHAPTER FIVE
Sabotage ... ?

Next up for Mira and Dave was the Magical Mystery Pouch Race.

"Here's your Magical Mystery Pouch!" said Miss Glitterhorn, handing Mira a large sack. It turned out that the Magical Mystery Pouch Race was a sack race.

Mira thought she should be okay with this one, since even Dave wouldn't eat a sack. In fact he looked comfortable when he first got into it. But then he wiggled along the ground in the sack like a big slug, and Mira couldn't help but laugh.

Dave was doing his Dave laugh, which was a sort of deafening singsong neigh. And that made Mira laugh more. So Dave laughed louder. And louder. And louder. Mira stopped laughing. (It wasn't THAT funny.) Dave was laughing so much that his eyes were popping out of his head. Sometimes Dave would get hysterically hungry, so Mira wondered if this was happening now.

"Are you feeling okay?" said Mira. Then
something fluttered past her eye. It had come
from the sack. She bent down and
picked up . . . a feather. Then another
feather fell out of the sack. Mira
looked closer.

The sack was packed full of feathers.

"THAT'S why you're laughing,"
said Mira. "You're being tickled!"

"Hee HAAAAAA hehe
HAAAAAAAA," guffawed Dave.

Mira helped Dave out of the sack and
brushed the feathers off him. Gradually his
laughter slowed and then stopped. Dave looked
relieved.

Mira realized she could still hear laughter.
She looked around and saw Yasmin, Sarah, and
other members of Team Sloth and their unicorns
all rolling around on the ground while the sack
racers from the other teams sped past them.

Miss Hind yelled at them for messing around
and gave them zero points. She said they must
have been hanging out with pigeons before
the race, but Mira wasn't so sure ... Why were
strange things happening only to Team Sloth?

The teams gathered for the last of the fun
events: the Hoop-onto-the-Unicorn-Horn
Throw. Each child had to stand ten feet from
their unicorn and throw a hoop onto the
unicorn's horn.

"This is my FAVE event," said Darcy. She spun her chair around in a circle and then threw the hoop like an Olympic discus thrower. Her unicorn, Star, pirouetted and caught the hoop neatly on her horn. The rest of Team Lions or Tigers broke out into wild applause and started cheering their names.

Mira clapped, too. She sort of wished she were on Darcy's team. Raheem reached into the bucket of hoops and screamed.

"Miss Hind!" he said. "The hoops—"

"Stop *moaning*, Sloths!" snapped Madame Shetland.

Mira looked in the bucket. Instead of hoops, there was a pile of unicorn poop.

"Hey, guys!" said Flo, arriving at the starting line. "Oh, why have you brought a bucket of poop?"

"We didn't!" said Mira. "Do you think the hoops are underneath?"

"Should we just throw them?" said Flo. Unicorn poop was small, neat, and glittery, so there were worse things you could throw.

"So. Gross." Raheem shook his head as he pulled the sleeve of his smelly PE closet tracksuit over his hand and pulled the tracksuit collar over his mouth.

Mira picked up some of the poop and waved it at the unicorns, just so it wouldn't be a shock. Sparkles nodded excitedly, Brave remained rooted to the spot, and Dave just shrugged.

"Ready ... set ...," called Miss Hind, raising her whistle to her lips.

SCRREEEEEEEEEEEEEEECHHH!

"Fantastic throwing, everyone!" shouted Miss Glitterhorn from the sidelines. "WAIT! Mira, Raheem, and Flo ... WHAT ON *EARTH* ARE YOU THROWING?!"

The event was restarted with a fresh set of hoops for Team Sloth. There were plenty of grumbles from the other teams, who thought it was probably Dave who had pooped in the bucket in the first place. Mira knew he didn't though— Dave would happily admit it if he did something like that. Also, Dave's poops weren't as small and neat and glittery as other unicorns'.

After everyone had had a turn at the fun events, the scores were counted up. Team Sloth had managed to get some points on the board, but they were still WAY behind the other teams. And Mira couldn't help but think that all the problems with the equipment had happened only to them. Something strange was going on . . .

"Raheem," she whispered, as they headed back to the school for some rainbow juice and glitter cookies. "I think . . . I think someone might be trying to stop us from doing well at field day. So many weird things have happened to our team!"

"Hang on a minute . . . ," said Raheem. "Do you mean sabotage?"

Before Mira could respond, there came a loud **"HA!"** from behind them. Mira knew exactly who that laugh came from.

"As if anyone would bother to *sabotage* you!" said Rani, as she caught up with them. Angelica trotted alongside Rani and gave an amused whinny.

Mira folded her arms. "So it's just a coincidence

65

that OUR clock stopped and OUR eggs were broken and OUR sacks had feathers in them and WE were given a bucket of poop? ALL OF THAT is just a coincidence?"

"It is statistically unlikely," confirmed Raheem.

Mira narrowed her eyes at her sister. Rani narrowed hers back. Then Angelica narrowed her eyes at Dave. Then Dave stuck out his tongue.

"Just accept it," said Rani. "Team Sloth are LOSERS!"

As Rani and Angelica smugly strutted away, Mira very much wished she still had that bucket of unicorn poop.

CHAPTER SIX
The Serious Sports Events

TEAM COBRA	TEAM LIONS OR TIGERS	TEAM RHINO	TEAM SLOTH
75	63	84	12

"It's ANYONE'S game!" Miss Glitterhorn grinned, as the whole school stood back out on the sports field. "I really think that any of the

teams could be our winners!"

"Really, Miss Glitterhorn, don't give them false hope," muttered Madame Shetland. "Now! It's time for the serious sports events. This will really test your partnership with your unicorn—especially the Uni-Pole Vault."

There were worried whispers from the younger members of the teams. Mira could see that even Rani and Jake gave each other a LOOK.

"But don't worry—just give it your best shot!" said Miss Glitterhorn.

Mira glanced at Dave. She got the feeling he wasn't looking forward to the serious sports events. When Miss Hind had blown her whistle to signal the end of snack time, Dave had tried

to distract everyone by pointing at something in the sky with his hoof and then running off. Mira found him hiding in a sparklebush.

The first event was the Long Jump. The unicorn and their rider would gallop along the track. When they reached the big white line, they would jump and see how far into the glitter-sandpit they landed. The results were very mixed—and it was clear that these events were much harder. Jake's unicorn, Pegasus, put one hoof over the white line, and the jump didn't count, despite Team Rhino's protests. Darcy and Star jumped very far, but then they bowed and did a celebratory tap dance and were docked points for getting glitter-sand in people's eyes.

Soon Mira and Dave were up—the first to jump from Team Sloth. Mira hopped onto Dave's back, and he walked over to the start of the runway. *So far, so good!* thought Mira.

Dave backed up a few steps.

"That's great, Dave," said Mira. "Get a longer run-up!"

Then he backed up a few more steps.

And a few more.

And a few more.

Mira realized he was actually just walking backward, away from the glitter-sandpit.

"Come on, Dave. You can do this! I believe in you!" She ruffled his mane.

Dave kept walking backward. "AND," Mira

continued, "I saved you some cookies from snack time . . ."

Dave stopped walking backward. His little ears pricked up, and he gave a grunt. Then he started trotting forward toward the track.

"That's it, Dave!" said Mira, giving him a pat. "Think of the cookies!"

Dave sped up. Mira could see the track approaching, leading up to the white line and the glitter-sandpit. But there was something else there, too. Something . . . yellow. Mira realized with a gulp that it was a banana peel—and Dave was going to slip on it!

"No—Dave! Stop!" she called. But Dave seemed to be thinking only of the cookies, and

he got faster, not slower! "Dave! Watch out for the bananAAAAAAAAARRRRRGGGGGGGHH!"

Dave skidded on the banana peel and shot forward. He and Mira were propelled through the air. Mira squeezed her eyes shut, hugged Dave's neck, and braced herself for the landing. Dave hadn't even had the chance to jump correctly, but all that mattered now was that they were both okay. At least the glitter-sand would be soft, she hoped.

They landed with a *thump*—the glitter-sand *was* soft—but it also wasn't very sandy and was a bit . . . leafy?

Mira opened her eyes. They were in a sparklebush. She saw Dave had his eyes closed, too. He opened one eye and looked at Mira.

"Oh dear—we didn't even make the glitter-sandpit!" she said.

"No—you jumped PAST it!" squeaked Flo, arriving at the bush on Sparkles and peering through the leaves.

"It's a school record!" said Raheem, beaming. The rest of Team Sloth were whooping and cheering behind them.

Mira and Dave were awarded twenty points

for their jump, even though Rani and Jake complained that the rules said your jump would be measured in the glitter-sandpit—so jumping past it shouldn't count.

Jake was still muttering about it when Raheem went up to take his jump. "They obviously didn't *mean* to do an amazing jump," he grumbled. "It must have been an accident."

Mira thought of the banana peel . . . so she looked over at the track—and there was another one! She told Miss Glitterhorn, who made Raheem and Brave wait until it was removed.

"How strange," said her teacher.

Mira looked over at her sister, who was standing with Angelica, very close to the runway. Rani saw her looking and mouthed, "WHAT?" Mira mouthed back, "NOTHING." But she didn't look away and watched Rani like a hawk for the rest of the Long Jump, even though Rani was mouthing, "WHY ARE YOU STARING AT ME?" and "YOU'RE SO WEIRD."

The rest of Team Sloth did their jumps, and they managed to get some more points. And no more banana peels appeared. *Interesting*, Mira thought.

Then it was time for the Uni-Pole Vault. It was a *really* hard event, and only a few people had managed to do it before Mira and Dave stepped up for their turn.

"It doesn't matter if we can't do it, Dave," she said, giving him a pat. "You already did a fantastic Long Jump!"

Dave looked at her with a twinkle in his eye. And then he winked.

"Okay . . . ," said Mira, feeling slightly uncertain. She climbed onto Dave's back and picked up a pole from the pile marked TEAM SLOTH.

Dave turned his head, grabbed the pole in his mouth, and ate it.

"Um, Dave, I think the pole is pretty important," said Mira. But Dave had already started his run-up. Mira looked up at the Uni-Pole Vault bar. It was dizzyingly high. How on earth would they get up there?

As if he was answering her question, Dave suddenly ducked low and kicked his back legs up, springing off the ground. Mira slid forward and clung to his neck. Together they turned a somersault in the air—and hurtled back toward the ground.

BBOOIIIIIIIIINNNGGG!!

For the second time that day, Mira shut her eyes and braced herself . . . Dave had BOUNCED on his HORN and they were now soaring up into the sky, turning somersaults as they went! They flew higher and higher—past the Uni-Pole Vault bar! Mira felt her stomach drop as they started to fall, still turning over and over . . .

And with a *THUD*, they landed on the spongy crash mat.

The cheers and applause from Team Sloth were deafening. Darcy's team cheered, too, and some of Team Cobra joined in. The teachers agreed that it was the most impressive Uni-Pole Vault they'd ever seen and awarded Mira and Dave forty points.

Team Rhino surrounded Miss Glitterhorn.

"But—but!" cried Jake. "They didn't use the pole!" He pointed at the pile of Team Sloth poles. Dave was standing over them and sniffing. He carefully nudged one of the poles away from the pile with his nose. Then Mira realized he was eating that one, too! She rushed over, thinking that it was not the best thing for Dave's stomach,

and pulled what remained of the pole out of his mouth.

But it wasn't plastic and metal—it was sticky and—Mira sniffed it—sugary. She tentatively licked it. It wasn't a Uni-Pole Vault pole at all—it was a giant candy cane.

They inspected the rest of the poles in Team Sloth's pile—they were ALL candy canes.

"Those are branches from the sugar trees," said Miss Glitterhorn, shaking her head. "They grow nearby—but I don't know what they're doing here! Borrow Team Rhino's poles and gather together the candy canes."

"We can't do that," said Raheem. "Dave's eaten them all."

Dave turned to face them and let out a thundering fart.

Some of the other Team Sloth unicorns copied Dave's Uni-Pole Vault technique, and Team Sloth racked up more points. Everyone held their breath as they watched the scoreboard.

TEAM COBRA	TEAM LIONS OR TIGERS	TEAM RHINO	TEAM SLOTH
91	60	103	103

"YAAAAAAAAAY!" cheered Team Sloth, all sharing a hug and high-fiving. Lots of them asked

Mira if they could give Dave a well-done pat.

Mira's chest was fizzing with excitement—they were tied for first with Team Rhino! And what's more, everyone was cheering for Dave!

"You were amazing, Dave," she said, scratching him behind the ears. "I'm so glad you're my Unicorn Best Friend Forever."

Dave shrugged and snorted, but Mira could see his cheeks turn pink.

CHAPTER SEVEN
Sneaker Stealing!

The teams filed back into the school for lunch.
Miss Glitterhorn told them all to leave their
sneakers in the PE locker room so they wouldn't
get mud in the cafeteria. Mira carefully laid her
glitter sneakers on the floor underneath her coat
hook. She'd tried really hard not to get them
muddy.

Mira was so excited she could hardly eat. But
she knew she would need lots of energy for the
Cross-Country Obstacle Race. Dave was also
excited, but he was always excited at lunchtime.

Darcy and Freya came over to sit with them. Freya soon had to leave because she was summoned to the girls' bathroom by her unicorn, Princess, who was devastated that competing in all the sports had messed up her mane.

"Go, Dave!" said Darcy. "What an awesome Uni-Pole Vault!"

Mira beamed with pride, though she could tell Dave wasn't used to being the center of attention. He shrugged and focused on his food.

"What do you think the obstacles will be?" said Darcy. "I just hope it's something DANGEROUS and not boring old cones and bits of rope."

"I hope it is boring old cones and bits of rope," said Raheem firmly.

Mira looked over at a table nearby, where Team Rhino were talking tactics.

"Dave did pretty well in the serious sports events," said one girl.

"That was a fluke!" hissed Jake. "And now it's a *race*—he won't go very fast on those stumpy legs!"

Mira was about to turn to Dave and say that they seemed to have Team Rhino worried, when she realized something. Rani wasn't there. Mira thought she'd be leading the team talk . . . Mira looked around at the other tables. Rani was nowhere to be seen. Where WAS she?

ᘮᘮᘮ

After lunch the teams all went back to the PE locker room to get their sneakers.

Mira went to her coat hook—and then stared

down at the floor in disbelief.

HER GLITTER SNEAKERS WERE GONE.

"Are you okay?" said Raheem, as Mira

desperately searched under the other hooks.

More of Team Sloth gathered around as Mira explained about the sneakers. They helped her look, but no one could find the sneakers anywhere. Students from other teams joined in the search.

Miss Hind came in to find out where the kids were. "Come on, it's time for the Cross-Country Obstacle Race. No stragglers!" she barked.

"We can't go yet. Mira's sneakers are missing!" said Raheem.

Miss Hind sighed and looked at her watch. Then Miss Glitterhorn and Madame Shetland came in, wondering what the holdup was.

"You'll just have to borrow some spare sneakers, Mira," said Miss Glitterhorn kindly. "We'll look for them later."

"But . . . ," said Mira, worried she might cry. Her parents had gotten the sneakers for her birthday as a special surprise because they saw her looking at them in the store window. She blinked back tears. Then she felt a nudge, followed by a scratchy mane and a warm nose nuzzling under her chin. It was a Dave hug!

"You can get some stinky lost-and-found sneakers to match your stinky PE outfit!" said a voice.

"Rani!" said Miss Glitterhorn.

Mira turned to look at her sister, who had a big grin on her face. Rani was wearing her own glitter sneakers, and she stuck out her right foot and wiggled it in Mira's direction. Mira snapped. She'd had enough!

"Rani STOLE my sneakers!" she shouted, pointing at her sister. "She's been playing tricks on Team Sloth all day—and SABOTAGING US!"

There was a stunned silence.

Rani was staring at her, openmouthed. "No. I . . ."

"Mira, this is a very serious accusation," said

Madame Shetland. "I would think very carefully about what you're saying."

"Where's your proof?" said Jake.

"I . . . well . . ." Mira looked down at the ground. She hadn't actually seen Rani do anything. But she had been really mean to Team Sloth. AND she'd made that speech, saying "do anything you can to win." AND she wasn't anywhere to be seen at lunch, right when the sneakers went missing. It MUST be her!

Then something interrupted her thoughts. It was a strange snuffling, grunting sound . . .

They all turned to look. Dave had his nose to the floor and seemed to be licking something. Then he trotted forward.

"Dave, don't lick the floor!" said Mira, running over to him.

"Gross," said someone from Team Rhino.

But then Mira looked closer. "Wait . . . ," she said. "I think Dave's found something." She saw that he was vacuuming up a trail of glitter that led out of the locker room door.

"It's a clue!" cried Mira, as she followed Dave.

"We don't have time for that now, Mira," said Miss Glitterhorn.

"I'll be quick! I promise!" Mira called behind her.

"Well, make sure you are. No—Team Sloth, that doesn't mean you can ALL go. Or you, Team Rhino! Everybody stay still! Okay, well we'll all just go for a little bit. Back in a moment, Madame Shetland!"

Miss Glitterhorn jogged ahead of the large crowd of children, all following Mira and Dave and the glitter trail. Dave kept on licking up the glitter all the way into the stable yard. And all the way up to one of the stables. All the stable doors had a wooden

sign with the unicorn's name, but on this door the sign was nearly hidden by all the pictures and hand-drawn posters that were stuck all over it.

"But . . . ," said Rani, as Dave, still eating the glitter, pushed the door open with his nose.

There, nestled among the hay, were Mira's glitter sneakers.

There was a shocked gasp from all the teams. Flo fainted. Miss Glitterhorn shook her head. "Rani . . . ," she said, sounding disappointed.

"I—I didn't take them!" said Rani.

"Yeah RIGHT," said Mira. "Where were you at lunch, then? You weren't in the cafeteria with your team."

"I—I was—" stammered Rani.

"You were SNEAKER STEALING!" said

Mira. She felt a bit giddy and wasn't sure if it was anger or triumph.

"No! I was with Mrs. Fetlock," said Rani.

Mrs. Fetlock oversaw Class Orange and was also the school's math teacher.

"How come?" said Mira.

"I'm doing extra work with her," said Rani, looking at her feet.

"Why would you do that?" blurted out Darcy, clearly horrified at the idea of voluntarily doing extra work.

"Because I'm behind, OKAY!" snapped Rani.

"Don't worry, Rani," interrupted Miss Glitterhorn. "There's nothing wrong with getting a little bit of help when you need it."

Mira could see Rani blinking furiously,
which she did on the VERY rare occasions
when she was about to cry. A tight feeling
twisted in Mira's stomach. She felt AWFUL.

Raheem handed her the glitter sneakers.
"Thanks, Raheem," she said glumly, and
she sat down to put them on. There were
strands of unicorn mane caught in the laces,
but otherwise they were as good as new.

"Well, it seems like this is all cleared up," said Miss Glitterhorn.

"Apart from why Mira's sneakers were in a stall?" said Yusuf.

"Mira probably put them there to FRAME Rani," said one of Rani's friends.

"Now, now, let's all stop accusing one another of things and get back to field day," said Miss Glitterhorn firmly, striding back through the stable yard. The children followed her. Mira's stomach twisted even tighter, and she sped up to walk alongside her sister.

"Rani . . . ," she said.

Rani turned around. "Just leave me alone!"

Rani's friend put her arm around her protectively, and Angelica snorted angrily at Mira.

"It's not your fault—you didn't know," said Raheem kindly, appearing at Mira's side.

Flo popped up between them. "Why don't we go win Unicorn School Field Day?"

Dave trumpeted a fart of agreement, and they all grinned. Mira followed Team Sloth out to the sports field, trying to ignore the guilty feeling in her chest. But it still didn't make sense—how DID her sneakers get in the stables?

CHAPTER EIGHT
Into the Forest...

"ON YOUR MARKS!"

Team Sloth were on their unicorns at the starting line of the Cross-Country Obstacle Race.

"GET SET!"

They could hear the shouts of Team Cobra, who'd set off a few minutes before. The teams were going one by one.

"GO!"

Brave shot off at a thundering gallop with Raheem clinging to his neck for dear life. The rest of Team Sloth trotted after him,

and Mira soon found herself at the back. She felt bad for thinking it, but maybe Jake did have a point about Dave's little legs.

The race would take them out to the farthest fields in the school grounds (and from the splashes they'd heard, part of it went through the swimming pool). Then back to the sports field, where they'd wait for the last team to arrive and then all complete the final dash to the finish line.

Team Sloth went up over a hill and followed a big red arrow into a field, where they weaved in and out of some cones. Another arrow pointed them to the next field, where there was a set of monkey bars. It didn't seem too hard so far.

They reached the end of the second field, where a path forked in two. The big red arrow pointed to the path on the left. On the arrow was scrawled THIS WAY. Brave, still leading the group, strode along the left path.

"Wait!" called Yusuf. "Doesn't that lead to the forest?"

Brave stopped abruptly, and all of Team Sloth collided with one another.

"The arrow was definitely pointing this way, though," said Ali.

Team Sloth all looked at one another.

"I think we should go back," said Raheem, patting Brave on the neck. Mira knew why he was saying it. The forest was full of sparkle spiders, and only Mira, Raheem, and Darcy knew that Brave was terrified of spiders.

"But if we turn back now, we might not finish the race at all," said one of the Toms.

"Should we just find the first obstacle and see what it's like?" said Sarah. The other team members voiced their agreement.

They walked farther and farther into the forest.

"I think I've found the obstacle!" called Anja.

The rest of Team Sloth caught up and saw what Anja was pointing at. It was a rickety rope bridge hanging over a swamp.

"It looks pretty dangerous," said Sarah.

"I'm sure it's . . . fine," said Anja uncertainly.

They paused for a moment as everyone
thought, and then they all started talking at once.

"Come on, let's just do it!"

"We're running out of time!"

"Are those piranhas?"

"Maybe we have to weave in and out of those flesh-eating plants over there?"

"HEY!" The noise paused, and Team Sloth looked over in surprise to see that it was Raheem who had yelled. He had climbed up onto a rock. "Arguing isn't going to get us anywhere," said Raheem. "We'll take a vote. And whatever the vote decides, we do—no arguing!"

"How about the ones who want to do the obstacle keep going, and the ones who are too scared go back?" said Anja.

Raheem shook his head. "We should stick together. No one on Team Sloth gets left behind."

Mira felt a huge surge of pride for her friend, and she could see that Brave felt the same. He

was standing next to Raheem with his head
held high, even though his eye was twitching
and he kept looking around for spiders.

"So," said Raheem. "Who wants to stay in
the forest and cross the terrifying rickety bridge
obstacle?"

Flo put her hand up and so did Anja and a
few others. Mira's hand moved—she wanted to
keep going and tackle the obstacle—but then she
looked at Raheem and Brave. Even though they
definitely didn't want to stay in the forest, they
were still making sure that everyone got a say. *That*
was good teamwork. Mira kept her hand down.

"Who wants us to find our way out of the forest?"

Raheem put his own hand up, Brave put his

hoof up, and other hands went up, including

Yusuf's, Sarah's, and Flo's.

"You can't really vote for both options,"

Mira said to Flo, as she put her hand up.

"But I'd be happy with both," said Flo.

Raheem counted the hands three times to make sure. Then he announced the result: "We are going to find our way out of the forest!" Most of Team Sloth, even the ones who had voted for the rickety bridge, looked relieved.

They turned back the way they came—only to find there was not one path leading back, but lots of paths, all leading in different directions.

Somewhere nearby a bird shrieked and something rustled, making them all jump.

Suddenly, Unicorn School felt very far away . . .

CHAPTER NINE
Unicorns Pointing North

"We're lost!" said Jimmy, as his unicorn snorted nervously.

"It's okay," said Raheem. "We'll just use our emergency fanny packs."

Mira looked at him. "Raheem, we don't have emergency fanny packs."

"Really?" said Raheem. "It's my dad's motto: *Never leave the house without your emergency fanny pack.*" He rolled up his lost-and-found tracksuit top and unzipped a blue fanny pack. "I always

carry an emergency map, an emergency pencil case, emergency socks, and an emergency cookie." Raheem jumped when he saw Dave had suddenly appeared next to him. "I'll just use this protractor to divide the cookie into—oh, Dave ate it."

Raheem unfolded his map and studied it. "Okay," he said. "So we just have to head north, and in about ten minutes, we should come out by the sports field."

"Hooray!" cheered Team Sloth. Jimmy patted Raheem on the back and said, "Let's go!"

No one moved.

"Which way is north?" said Ali.

"Um . . ." Raheem's face fell. The Toms sighed.

"The unicorns will tell us," said Flo, who was furiously brushing Sparkles's mane.

They all looked at her. "What?" said Raheem.

Flo looked up. "They point north."

"What do you mean?" said Mira.

"If you leave them standing on their own for a bit, they point north," Flo explained. "Sparkles is always doing it."

Everyone looked unsure, but they climbed off the unicorns, moved back a few paces, and waited. The unicorns just stared back at them.

"This is silly . . . ," Anja started to say, but she trailed off. The unicorns were starting to move. They shuffled and turned around in a circle. Then they stopped. All the horns were pointing

in the same direction. Even Dave's! "Hooray!" cheered Team Sloth for the second time. The children hopped back onto their unicorns, and they all started down the path that led north.

As they rode along, they sang songs and made up Team Sloth chants. Mira stroked Dave's tufty mane and smiled to herself. Team Sloth might not win—but they were having the BEST time, AND they were working together as a team.

"You were great, Raheem!" she said, as Brave trotted up next to her and Dave.

"Thanks!" Raheem grinned. "I bet you'll be getting yourself an emergency fanny pack now."

"Yeah," said Mira (thinking she probably wouldn't).

Team Sloth cheered again as they emerged from the forest. They could see the sports field, with the other three teams lined up near a table of juice and cookies. The teachers were looking around and checking their watches, obviously wondering where Team Sloth had gotten to.

"There they are!" someone called.

As they arrived at the table, Madame Shetland marched toward them.

"Where have you BEEN, Team Sloth?"

"We turned back at the flesh-eating plants, and the unicorns pointed us home," said Flo.

"I beg your pardon?" said Madame Shetland.

"We had trouble finding the obstacles," said Raheem.

"Well, I'm not sure how you managed that when there were enormous signs to show you the way," Madame Shetland said.

"We—" said Mira, but before she could tell her that it was the enormous signs that had pointed them into the forest, the principal had spun on her heels and started marching back toward the refreshments table.

Darcy wheeled over with Star trotting alongside. "You guys are in the final dash with Team Rhino!" she said.

"WHAT?" said Mira.

"Really?!" said Raheem.

"Yes!" said Darcy. "Team Lions or Tigers won the Cross-Country Obstacle Race, so Sloths and Rhinos are still tied for first place!"

Mira couldn't believe they had reached the final. When they'd turned back in the forest, she

thought all was lost. "Well done on winning the Cross-Country, Darcy!" she said.

Darcy waved her hand. "Oh, it was super easy. Just boring old cones and bits of rope. Nothing dangerous at all—SO pathetic. Plus, I told my team that all the obstacles were electrified so they had to go really quickly."

"Team Sloth and Team Rhino, line up for the final dash!" bellowed Miss Hind.

Team Rhino were ready, and their unicorns were snorting and stamping their feet impatiently. At the other end of the field, in the distance, was the finish line *and* the trophy cabinet.

Mira looked around for Dave. She saw with despair that he'd fallen asleep underneath the

refreshments table with his head in the cookie
bucket.

"Dave!" she said, poking him. "Quick—
we've got to race!" Dave lifted his head—it was
completely stuck in the bucket.

Brave whinnied. He was getting impatient, too.
Mira saw that Raheem had decided to completely
unlace and re-lace his sneakers. "Just making sure
they fit exactly right," he said cheerily.

Brave sighed.

"ON YOUR MARKS!"

Mira looked at Brave. He was easily the fastest
unicorn on their team.

"GET SET . . ."

Mira looked at Dave. He was staggering

around, knocking over people and jugs of rainbow juice with his bucket head.

She remembered Jake at lunch talking about Dave's stumpy legs. And Rani talking about him being the world's awfulest unicorn.

Wouldn't it be nice to stand a chance of winning, just once?

GGGGoooOOOOOOOO!!

"Raheemdoyouwanttoswapunicorns?" said Mira quickly.

"What?" said Raheem. He'd still only re-laced half of one shoe.

Mira ran over to Brave and jumped onto his back. She heard a loud *POP* and turned to see

that Dave had pulled his head out of the bucket.
He saw Mira, and his ears and tail drooped.

"Dave, it's okay—we're going to win!" she said,
and she patted Brave's neck. "Go, Brave! Let's
win this for Team Sloth!" Brave gave a surprised
whinny, but he shot forward into a gallop.

The wind blew through Mira's hair, and

everything whooshed past in a blur. They were going so fast! Soon they reached the front of the pack of unicorns, with only Jake and Pegasus ahead of them. And then they were neck and neck. And then they edged into the lead. The finish line was getting closer and closer— they were going to win!

And then she heard a whinny she knew very well.

Mira looked over her shoulder.

Way back, near the starting line, Raheem and Dave were trotting along. Raheem gave Mira a thumbs-up, and Dave gave a snort.

Mira looked at the finish line and then back at Raheem and Dave. She looked at Jake and

Pegasus, edging nearer to them again. "Watch your back!" called Jake smugly.

And Mira knew what she had to do.

Mira nudged Brave so that he wheeled around in a circle. At first he tried to turn around again, but then he saw Raheem. Brave gave a happy neigh and started to gallop toward him.

There were shouts of surprise from the other riders as Mira and Brave passed them, going the wrong way.

Raheem and Dave looked equally surprised when they reached them.

"But, Mira—you were going to win!" said Raheem.

"Everyone should finish the race on their own

UBFF," said Mira. "That's more important than winning. No one on Team Sloth gets left behind."

There was a loud sniff, and Mira saw that Brave was wiping a tear from his eye with his hoof. Raheem's face broke into a smile. "Are you sure?"

Mira grinned at him. "Of course!"

They swapped unicorns.

"Remember, Brave—slow and steady wins the race." Brave rolled his eyes, but Mira could see he was happy to be reunited with his HBFF. They set off painfully slowly.

Dave gave Mira a nudge with his nose, which was his way of saying he was happy to be back with her, too. She hopped onto his back, and the plump little unicorn stamped his foot.

"Okay, Dave—let's do this!" said Mira. "Go, Team Sloth!"

Dave set off as fast as his little legs would carry him.

In completely the wrong direction.

CHAPTER TEN
The Mystery Quest

Madame Shetland stood at the front of the Great Hall. All the children sat with their teams for the prize-giving ceremony.

"Tied in third place, we have Team Cobra and Team Lions or Tigers," said the principal. "With a special mention for Darcy, from Class Red, who I am told really motivated her team through the Cross-Country Obstacle Race."

"WHOOP! WHOOP!" called Darcy, and her team cheered, although several flinched. Both

teams went up to the stage to collect their medals and high-fived one another.

"In second place we have Team Sloth," said Madame Shetland.

Mira's team went wild, cheering, hugging, and high-fiving as they went up to collect their medals. When they returned to their seats, Mira grinned at Dave. She didn't mind about not winning. They'd gotten to the final, *and* she'd finished the race on her UBFF!

"I'm sorry I abandoned you for a moment, Dave," she said.

Dave shrugged. But Mira could tell he was still a little upset. Luckily she'd been able to sneak back to her dorm room and get something . . .

"Why don't you take a look in your lunch box?" Mira said, sliding it over to him.

Dave looked up at her in surprise, and with a swift horn movement he opened the lunch box. It was full of doughnuts again!

"I brought spares." Mira smiled at her unicorn, who was happily munching away. Now she knew she was definitely forgiven!

"And now," said Madame Shetland, "the winners of Unicorn School Field Day—with a special mention for Jake and Pegasus, whose brilliant final dash clinched the victory for them—Team Rhino!"

Madame Shetland led the applause as Jake and Rani's team walked up to the front of the Great

Hall to get their winners' medals and lift the trophy. Miss Hind threw open the trophy cabinet.

The trophy was tiny. And it seemed to be made from a couple of egg cartons sprayed gold.

Team Rhino looked disappointed. But not for long, because soon it would be time to reveal the mystery quest.

Just then something tumbled out of the trophy

cabinet. It was a pile of rainbow tracksuits!

"How did they get in *there*?" said Raheem.
Mira shook her head—SO many things hadn't
made sense today.

Miss Glitterhorn brought the tracksuits over
and sat down next to Team Sloth. "Never mind,
Team Sloth—you did very well."

"Yes, Miss Glitterhorn—we tried our best," said
Anja.

"And some of those obstacles were very tricky."
Their teacher smiled at them all.

"I know—we didn't even do the rickety
swamp bridge!" said Flo.

"Yes, the—what?" Miss Glitterhorn looked
confused.

"The rickety bridge. Over the piranha swamp. In the middle of the forest," said Flo.

Miss Glitterhorn got them to explain. She said that the obstacle course had NOT gone through the forest—the route went through the fields. "Didn't you follow the big red arrows?" she said.

"We did—they pointed into the forest," said Raheem.

Miss Glitterhorn went over to talk to the other teachers. Then Madame Shetland walked back over to the front of the hall.

"It appears that there was an act of sabotage in the final event," said the principal gravely. "Someone moved the arrows to send Team Sloth into the forest. Anyone who knows anything

about this should speak up now."

There was a hushed silence around the hall.

Then a hand went up near where Mira was sitting.

"I found this next to one of the signs," said Anja, from Team Sloth. "I thought one of us had dropped it, but maybe it was the person who moved the sign?" She walked forward and handed something to Madame Shetland.

"Does anyone recognize this?" said Madame Shetland, holding up a fluffy pencil case.

Mira swallowed—she knew who it belonged to. But she didn't say anything. She remembered that the arrow pointing to the forest had THIS WAY scrawled on it. She had thought it didn't look quite right. AND it had been written in gel pen.

"Anyone?" said Madame Shetland.

"It's mine."

Rani walked forward. Murmurs echoed around the hall.

"So she WAS sabotaging you, Mira!" said Jimmy.

"I didn't move the signs, though—or do any of those other things," said Rani. "I swear!"

Madame Shetland looked at her. "Can you explain why your pencil case was found there?"

"I have no idea!" said Rani desperately.

Madame Shetland frowned. "Rani, I'm going to give you one more chance to tell me the truth."

Mira looked down at her feet. She didn't think her sister was lying. But what other explanation was there? Then she noticed that

there were still bits of unicorn mane in her laces.

WAIT A MINUTE!

Before she knew it, Mira was running to stand next to her sister. "Madame Shetland! Rani's telling the truth—she didn't do it!"

Rani's eyes met Mira's. Her expression was a mixture of gratitude and confusion.

Madame Shetland turned to Mira. "And what makes you say this, Mira?"

"Because I think I know who DID do it."

Madame Shetland raised her eyebrows and waited for Mira to continue.

"It was Angelica—her unicorn."

Rani's hand flew to her mouth. And then

she spun around to see Angelica's face. But Angelica was tiptoeing away from Team Rhino and toward the door.

"I think Angelica knew how much Rani wanted to win—so she tried to make sure it happened," Mira continued.

"Angelica?" said Rani, horrified.

The unicorn walked back to join Rani, hanging her head in shame.

"I think she just wanted to make you happy," said Mira. "I mean, I wanted to beat you, too!"

Mira thought about how desperate she'd been to beat her sister's team. So desperate that she'd abandoned her UBFF! Dave trotted over to join her, and Mira gave him a squeeze.

"Well," said Madame Shetland. "I don't feel that Team Rhino should lose out because of the actions of one of their team." There was a big sigh of relief from Team Rhino. Rani looked the most relieved—even though she hadn't known what Angelica was up to, Mira knew she would still feel bad that Angelica had done it for her.

"But Team Sloth *could* have won more points if they hadn't been sabotaged." Madame Shetland

paused for a moment. "I declare that Team Sloth are honorary joint winners—they will share the trophy. AND go on the mystery quest!"

There was a pause as this sunk in, then Team Sloth went wild!

They ran to the front of the hall, jumping up and down and singing the songs they'd made up on their trip back from the forest. They picked up Mira and Dave and got them to crowd-surf.

Team Rhino took it well. They were mostly pleased to still be going on the quest.

When her team eventually put her down, Mira looked around for her sister.

Rani was in the corner of the hall with Angelica and Madame Shetland.

"At least you're going on the quest!" said Mira.

"I'm not," said Rani.

"But you didn't do anything . . ." Mira looked from Rani to Madame Shetland.

"Angelica is going to spend tomorrow in detention," explained Madame Shetland. "I know she was trying to do a good thing for her human, but what she did put you all in danger. We simply can't allow her to go on the quest.

Rani has agreed to stay here with her."

Rani nodded. "It's fine," she said quietly.

Mira thought for a moment. Her sister was a pain, but she was still her sister. She thought of all the silly games they played at home (which Mira was banned from mentioning at Unicorn School on PAIN OF DEATH). And the way they had spent hours playing with their imaginary unicorns, years before they'd come to real Unicorn School. She didn't have fun with anyone like she did with Rani. And she knew how much Rani adored quests.

"You have to go," Mira said. "You can borrow Dave. I'll stay here."

Dave grunted in surprise.

Rani blinked. It looked like she had tears in her
eyes. "R–really?"

Both Mira and Rani looked at Madame
Shetland.

"It's an unusual solution," said the principal.
"But it has been an unusual day." She nodded.
"I can allow this."

"He has to have a bath and get his mane styled
before I'll be seen with him," said Rani, sounding
much more like her old self.

Mira looked at Dave, who shrugged. "Fine,"
said Mira.

"And I have one more demand," said Rani.

Mira sighed. She was getting a little annoyed
now—she was only trying to do something nice!

"And what is that, Rani?" said Madame
Shetland.

"I won't go on the quest unless Mira comes,
too."

∪ ∪ ∪

Early the next morning, Team Sloth and Team
Rhino (minus Angelica), gathered at the entrance
to the forest.

Mrs. Fetlock was handing out nets. Mira
and Rani had gone to see Angelica in her stall
before they left. They didn't want her to feel too
sad. But it turned out that Darcy and Star were
also in detention for customizing their rainbow
tracksuits (or "ruining them," according to
Madame Shetland), and they were already in her

stall and had offered to include her in their girl band. So they thought she'd be okay.

Mrs. Fetlock was explaining that the mystery quest was to collect rainbow light. They'd travel to the amazing Rainbow Hill, where they'd use their special nets to scoop the rainbow light from the sky. Then they'd bring it back to the darkest part of the Fearsome Forest and use it to light the forest lamps.

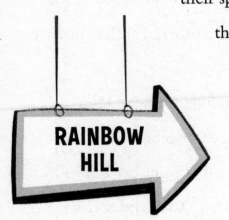

Everyone was VERY excited!

"You're HOGGING the unicorn, you hog!" grumbled Rani, fidgeting around and shoving Mira in the back.

"No, YOU are!" Mira wriggled backward. "And he's named Dave, not 'the unicorn.'"

"I want to go in the front," said Rani. "I can't see anything with your big head in the way."

"He's MY unicorn so I get to go in the front," said Mira.

Dave sighed and trotted forward with the rest of the unicorns as they went up the path. They could see the rainbow light glinting over the brow of the hill, creating multicolored, ever-changing patterns in the sky.

Mira and Rani didn't stop arguing ALL DAY.

But they still had the best quest EVER!

MISS GLITTERHORN'S GENERAL KNOWLEDGE QUIZ

How much do YOU know about Unicorn School?

1. How many classes are there at Unicorn School?
   a. 5 – A, B, C, D, and E
   b. 7 – One for each color of the rainbow: Red, Orange, Yellow, Green, Blue, Indigo, Violet
   c. 3 – Breakfast, Lunch, and Dinner

2. What is the official Unicorn School Field Day uniform?
   a. Pajamas
   b. Rainbow tracksuits
   c. Pink tank tops with rabbits on them

3. Who now holds the Unicorn School record for the Long Jump?
   a. Queen Boudiccorn
   b. Mira and Dave
   c. King Henry the Neighth

4. Which sport is NOT a real Unicorn School sport?
    a. Uni-Pole Vault
    b. Bungee Wrestling
    c. Egg-and-Spoonicorn Race

5. What class is Rani in?
    a. Class Indigo
    b. Class Yellow
    c. Class Red

Answers: If you got ...

Mostly As: Good try! Read this book again and see how many you get right next time!

Mostly Bs: You're top of the class. Gold medal to YOU!

Mostly Cs: Better luck next time! It's back to Unicorn School for you.

UNICORN JOKES

What do unicorns like to play in gym class?
Stable tennis

How do unicorns get to the park?
On a uni-cycle

What did the unicorn wear to school?
A uni-form

How do you know that a unicorn has been in your house?
It leaves glitter everywhere!

Why did the unicorn cross the road?
Because it wanted to see its NEIGHbors.

What's the difference between a unicorn and a carrot?
One is a funny beast and the other is a bunny feast!

Dave and Mira's story isn't ending! Everyone's favorite unicorn best friends will be back in *Dave the Unicorn: Dance Party!*

Turn the page for a sneak peek!

CHAPTER ONE
Back to Unicorn School!

It was a cloudy Tuesday afternoon and Mira was dancing around the kitchen with her cat, Pickles. Mira's older sister, Rani, rolled her eyes as she finished the after-dinner dishwashing (her chore for that week), and flicked water at Mira and Pickles as they twirled past the sink.

"Bleurgh!" spluttered Mira as a soap bubble landed in her mouth.

Rani dried her hands on a dish towel and snatched Pickles off Mira. "My turn! Okay,

Pickles, you can be my unicorn," she said. "I need to practice my moves for the school dance."

As Rani and Pickles swept past her, Mira had to admit that Rani was an annoyingly good dancer. Rani and her unicorn, Angelica, were annoyingly good at lots of things. The trophy shelf in their living room was full of all Rani's medals and trophies from winning tons of Unicorn School quests and competitions. Mira had just two medals so far.

Mira and Rani both went to Unicorn School. It was a magical place where students were matched with their Unicorn Best Friend Forever (UBFF) and had all kinds of brilliant quests and adventures!

It was almost time to go back to Unicorn School and Mira was BEYOND EXCITED to see her UBFF, Dave. He wasn't exactly how she'd imagined her perfect unicorn to be . . . he could be a little stubborn. And greedy. And he fell asleep in all their lessons. But they had so much fun together. And the school dance was going to be the most fun EVER. She couldn't imagine anything better in the entire world than spinning around the dance floor with Dave!

ᘁᘁᘁ

Later that night Mira lay in bed, too excited to sleep. She took out her diary from her bedside table and started thinking about all the awesome things she was going to do with Dave. *And* with

Darcy and Raheem—her two human best friends at Unicorn School.

Going on AMAZING quests

Dance with my BFFs

Midnight feasts in the dormitory

And BEST OF ALL... DAVE, MY UBFF!!!!

Thinking about Dave made Mira smile. He always made everything super fun, often in unexpected ways. Sure, he sometimes had to be bribed with snacks to do things. And sometimes he caused a teeny, tiny bit of havoc. *And* he held the Unicorn School record for most farts in class. But he didn't *mean* to misbehave. Dave was Mira's UBFF, and she loved him.

Mira tucked her diary back in the drawer and fell asleep.

∪ ∪ ∪

Mom usually took Mira and Rani to the Magic Portal where they could travel to Unicorn School— but today Dad was driving them, and they had to explain *everything* to him. He even nearly forgot to take them to the supermarket to buy treats for their unicorns! (Most unicorns liked carrots and hay, but Dave liked doughnuts best of all.)

"Stop, Dad!" yelled Mira. They were about to drive right past the Magic Portal in the rec center parking lot! Dad made an emergency stop as Mira hung out of the car, waving to her friend Raheem.

Rani refused to be seen dead (her words) with Mira at Unicorn School, so Mira had arranged to go through the portal with Raheem. He was just finishing the "Rules of Keeping Safe" song with his dad, but did wave back.

Dad was under strict instruction to take a picture of them before they went through the portal. Rani would only pose for a fraction of a second, but the photo of the back of her head would have to do.

"Bye, Dad!" Mira blew him a kiss through the car window and made sure she had her bag of unicorn treats. "Ready, Raheem? Why have you got your eyes closed?"

"I always feel sick going through the portal," Raheem said. "So I'm doing my calming breathing."

Mira grabbed his hand and pulled them both through the bushes. No matter how many times

she went through the portal, it never stopped
being absolutely, completely magical.

First, her toes started to tingle, then her legs
and arms, and then rainbow light burst all around
them and they were WHOOSHING through
the air before landing with a soft *thump* on the
Landing Haystack in the middle of the Grand
Paddock at Unicorn School.

"Wow," breathed Mira as she looked around.
It was autumn, and all the leaves in the Fearsome
Forest were turning gorgeous shades of red and
gold. Children were arriving in a steady stream
on the Landing Haystack and running to find their
UBFFs. The unicorns were grazing and playing in
the paddocks and fields around Unicorn School.

Mira could see their breath puffing in the chilly
air as she searched for Dave.

"Ta-daaaa!" a voice sang out behind them on
the haystack. Their friend Darcy launched off
the haystack and did a spectacular spin in her
wheelchair, with her arms in the air. "Did you
miss me?"

Mira laughed and ran over for a hug. "Of course I missed you. That was awesome!"

Darcy flicked her fluffy blond hair back over her shoulder. "I know," she said. "I've been practicing my moves for the school dance. I started a feet-and-wheels dance troupe at my other school, because I was kicked off the murderball team. They said I was too aggressive or something. Anyway, dance is WAY more my thing."

"What's murderball?" asked Raheem cautiously.

"It's like rugby but in wheelchairs. And more dangerous," Darcy replied, looking around for her unicorn, Star.

Raheem looked a little bit lost for words. "Shall we go find our unicorns?" he said.

Star and Brave were grazing in the Grand
Paddock and cantered over as soon as they
spotted Darcy and Raheem. Mira couldn't
see Dave.

"Is that him?" asked Darcy, pointing to a giant
pile of straw by the side of the fence. Some of the
Unicorn School teachers were standing around
it, poking something on the top of the straw pile
with a stick. Mira looked closer and saw that it
was a small unicorn curled up, fast asleep.

"Wake up!" yelled the PE teacher, Miss Hind.

"How is he still asleep?" muttered another
teacher, shaking his head.

"He's been up there for sixteen hours!"
said their class teacher, Miss Glitterhorn.

Dave farted loudly in his sleep.

Mira gave a huge smile. *There* was her UBFF. And she knew JUST how to wake him up!

That's all we have room for, but
Dave the Unicorn: Dance Party keeps
going after that—we promise!

And keep an eye out for the fourth
book in the series,
Dave the Unicorn: Field Trip!

PIP BIRD

is a children's author living in London. When she's not writing magical stories, she dreams of going to Unicorn School and having her own unicorn best friend.